SAMMY MAKES A FRIEND

By Heather D. Malboeuf
Illustrated, and edited, by Rob Sargeant

Weak & Foolish
Productions

The Land of Plenty

In the Land of Plenty there lived a hidden community of woodland animals dwelling in pockets of, as yet, untouched forest.

What were they hiding from? Can you guess?

They were hiding because humans had displaced many of the wild animals from their natural habitat. For the humans, in their quest to put down roots in the forested jewel called Comox, had cleared much of the forests; uprooting the woodland creatures that lived there, chasing away, or killing them.

In one of these forest pockets lived a most lowly and fearful creature named, Sammy.

Why was he fearful? Can you guess?

Sammy lived in a place he called the Big Woods. It was the most beautiful place in the world to him. Now, Sammy had spent a sheltered life in the Big Woods living his entire life there. It was his home. But he had constant fear that the humans would come to his home one day and clear the woods, leaving him homeless or worse, dead.

What was Sammy's favorite pastime? Can you guess?

Sammy's favorite pastime was eating, and there was one thing that Sammy liked to eat best of all.

What was it? Can you guess?

Sammy loved to eat delicious leaves. Once, Sammy tried eating a leaf with prickles but that didn't go so well.

What type of leaves did Sammy try to eat? Can you guess?

Sammy tried to eat a blackberry leaf, and blackberry bushes have prickles. Ouch!!

Did you guess that Sammy was a leaf eating type of forest animal? Let's see if you can guess what type of animal he was. Here's a clue. Wherever Sammy went, he left a trail behind.

What kind of trail was it? Can you guess?

A trail of slime.

What kind of animal was Sammy? Can you guess?

Did you guess that Sammy was a snail? No, he wasn't a snail. But that was a good guess, anyway. Sammy was a slug. Not an ordinary slug. Sammy was not-just-any-slug. He had style!

Why do you think that Sammy was stylish? Can you guess?

It's not because he wore a tuxedo or top hat. Sammy had style because wherever he traveled he purposefully left behind the initials S.T.S. written with his slime.

What did the initials mean? Can you guess?

The initials S.T.S. stood for Sammy The Slug. It was Sammy's monogram slug style.

Sammy was the most unique slug in the whole Comox Valley!

Family

Sammy lived with his father, Sam, and his mother, Vi. They loved him very much.

Sammy's dad was strong, adventurous, and spent all day exploring the valley, leaving Sammy alone with his mother for hours, as Sammy had no neighbors to play with.

His mom was very loving. She was a slug of few words, and had a quiet spirit. Sammy was very close to his mother. She was his only friend. They liked spending time together – eating! As much as Sammy loved his mother; he still wanted to grow up to be an explorer like his dear old dad, who was out every day looking for new slug habitat, in case they had to flee from theirs because of the humans. But Sammy was very lonely for a friend to play with. Sammy and his parents were the only animals living in the Big Woods, except for a visiting forest animal who came to his home one day leaving behind a different kind of trail.

What kind of animal was it? Can you guess?

Peter Cottontail

Sammy was alone at his home one day when he spotted an animal he had never seen before. His parents had described to him what a bunny looked like, so he guessed that this white, furry animal, with pink eyes, and very long ears, must be one.

Even though the bunny was much bigger than Sammy he hoped with all his heart that when it got up close to him it would stop and play. Sammy waited eagerly for the bunny to reach him so he could introduce himself, and ask the bunny to play. When it stopped beside Sammy he could hardly contain his excitement. Sammy thought for sure that it was going to play with him, but before Sammy could say anything, the bunny said something that dashed all Sammy's hopes and dreams.

What did the bunny say? Can you guess?

It said, in a female voice, "Ewww... a slug!" She turned up her nose at Sammy, and hopped away.

Sammy was very, disappointed. He was totally crushed; as he wanted a friend so desperately.

In honor of the first animal Sammy ever saw, he named the left behind trail, The Bunny Trail. Which it is still named to this very day.

The Little Woods

Next door to Sammy's home was a place, Sammy dubbed, The Little Woods. This was the place Sammy came to pray.

Now, Sammy prayed every day for two things:
1. Not, to lose his home, and,
2. To, make a friend.

This was also the place that Sammy came to dream, BIG DREAMS.

Sammy also loved to go to The Little Woods to listen to the birds singing high up in the trees. He found it peaceful, and calming, listening to them. It was not surprising then, that birds were Sammy's favorite animals. Very rarely did birds come down from up in the trees. But if one did, he would

slowly move closer to it to see how close he could get before it would fly away. Sammy never tired of this game. His favorite thing about birds was the sound their wings made as they flew over him. It filled him with such great joy.

When Sammy would leave his mother to go to the Little Woods she would always ask, "Where are you going Sammy?"

What do you think Sammy said? Can you guess?

Sammy would just say, "I'm going to The Little Woods." His mother never worried that she didn't know exactly where he went. She just trusted that he hadn't gone far.

In the rainy season a river, and waterfall, would form on the one side of The Little Woods. Sammy was fascinated by water, and loved to look at it, and relax.

Now how did the river, and the waterfall, appear to a human? Can you guess?

To a human the river was simply a creek, and the waterfall was nothing more than water rushing over the side of a ditch in a torrential rainfall. But to Sammy, a tiny slug, the creek seemed very wide, and the waterfall, very high. To Sammy they were huge! And while the river, and waterfall, flowed in The Little Woods, they were both his private paradise.

Slug School

Sammy's parents decided that, after Sammy had tried to eat prickly blackberry leaves, their son should go to slug school to learn what was safe for a slug to eat. The big day came for him to start his classes.

Sammy was so excited to go to his first day of school. *"Maybe I'll make a new friend at school today,"* he thought.

Sammy's mom walked with her son to his new school. She wanted to make sure that her son made it safely there.

The slug school was in the adjoining woods to their home. But slugs aren't known to be speedy; so it takes them a long time to go anywhere. And because of their small size, too, it takes them a long time to go a short distance. It seemed a very long distance for Sammy, and his mom, to travel. But finally they arrived.

Sammy was surprised to hear the fear in his mom's voice, when she said to him, suddenly, "Whatever you do

Sammy, don't go on the other side of that hedge!"

"What's a hedge?" asked Sammy.

"Do you see the trees, there in front of you, all close together in a row? It's man- made."

"Yes," said Sammy.

"The humans planted it as a barrier to keep us animals off their land. Humans live there."

"Okay," said Sammy, wondering why she was so afraid.

Then, Sammy heard a voice say, "You hoo… come over here."

Sammy and his mom moved toward the sound of the voice, until they saw, on the other side of a tree, was another yellow banana slug.

It was the teacher, Miss Selma. She warmly greeted Sammy and his mom."Hello Vi, this must be your son. It's nice to meet you, Sammy. Your mother has told me all about you, and how helpful you are at home."

Sammy was so nervous he didn't know what to say back to Miss Selma so he slid behind his mother to hide from Miss Selma.

"Are you shy, Sammy?" asked Miss Selma.

"Oh, he's just shy about meeting new slugs. You're the first slug Sammy has met other than his parents of course," said Vi.

Sammy's mom turned to Sammy and said, "Say "Hi Miss Selma," to your new teacher."

Sammy peered, hesitantly, around his mother, to take a better look at Miss Selma. He could see that Miss Selma was smaller than his mom, and she had a nice well-rounded shape for a slug. Also, she was moist too.

"Moist is good," thought Sammy.

"It's okay Sammy, I'm just a banana slug, like you; and us slugs need to stick together," said Miss Hoot. His teacher giggled at the joke she had just made.

Sammy giggled too. He decided that he liked Miss Selma a lot, because she was funny. So, to his mother's relief, and Miss Selma's delight, he said a weak, "Hi," back.

Then Miss Selma said, cheerfully, "Come along now Sammy, I'll introduce you to the other students."

Sammy had to be coaxed by his mother, to go with her, as he was afraid to leave his mother's side. "Go with Miss Selma, Sammy, it will be okay, I promise," said his mom, who smiled lovingly at him, and then waved good-bye.

Sammy didn't want to say good-bye to his mom.

"Bye Vi," said Miss Selma.

"Bye Miss Selma," said his mom.

Sammy followed his teacher closely, all the while with his eyes followed his mother as she left.

All of a sudden Miss Selma stopped, and Sammy slid forward into her backside with a thump! Sammy was so embarrassed. He couldn't say anything at all, but began to frantically move back, as fast as he could go. Sammy couldn't believe that he had bumped into his teacher.

"Oh, how embarrassing," thought Sammy.

Mercifully, Miss Selma pretended that she hadn't noticed Sammy's accidental bump. Instead she focused on quickly introducing Sammy to the other students, saying, "Class, I want you to meet Sammy, our new student."

She introduced each of the students to Sammy, one by one: this is Lyn, Divid, Tina, Di-Ann, Wayne, Rosie and Tom Tom.

"Say 'Hi' to Sammy students," said Miss Selma.

"Hi," they said in unison.

Sammy replied with a weak, "Hi," back to them. He looked more closely at the other students, and noticed that they were all yellow banana slugs, like himself, except for Tom Tom who was a brown color, with black spots.

At recess, Sammy watched the other slugs from a distance, not knowing, what to say or do, as he was afraid. Then he noticed Lady Di-Ann, was staring at him and blinking a lot. Her behavior, made Sammy very uncomfortable, which was noticed by Tina.

Tina said to Sammy "Oh. Di's just flirting with you Sammy. She flirts with all the new students. Don't pay her any attention."

Tina continued talking all the while, Sammy listened not saying anything back. He was just happy that one of the slug students was talking to him.

Tina rambled on, "She thinks she's so high and mighty, calling herself Lady Di-Anne. She also thinks she's the most attractive female slug here. Why I've seen her pretend to drop a leaf in front of a new slug so that he'll pick it up for her, just to get some attention. If she does that to you Sammy, don't fall for it. Just let her pick it up herself. She thinks she's so high-fa-lu-tin that male slugs should fall all over themselves to help her. Let her help herself, I say. She's a capable slug."

Sammy didn't know what to say to Tina, who was doing all the talking. Sammy wondered if she'd be his friend, and play with him, but he didn't know how to ask her. He thought he'd introduce himself in his unique way.

Sammy turned his back on Tina, who was still talking to him. Then he moved around wildly in front of her, leaving behind a message with his slime. Next, Sammy bravely turned around to face her. Tina stopped talking, quite surprised at what Sammy did.

"Gosh, what is - that?" said Tina to Sammy. But

before Sammy could answer her, the other slugs had gathered around to see Sammy's initials.

"What does 'STS' mean?" asked Divid.

"Sammy the slug," replied a proud, and smiling, Sammy.

Everyone was silent for a few seconds. Then Tom Tom spoke up. "I think it stands for Sammy the show-off!" Then Tom Tom laughed at Sammy, and everyone joined in laughing at Sammy.

Sammy was so humiliated and embarrassed that he didn't say anything back in response to Tom Tom's teasing.

Just then Miss Selma appeared to call her students back to class. Sammy was very grateful for the interruption, as he was having difficulty fitting in with the other students. Miss Selma said, "Let's go over the rules. No one go under the hedge to forage for food. There's plenty of food to eat in the school yard."

Sammy, feeling a little bold asked, "Why, because humans are there?"

"Humans," Lyn, fearfully stammered.

Miss Selma replied, "Yes."

Sammy not knowing anything about humans, except that they steal animal's homes, spoke up, asking,"What would happen if you did go under the hedge?"

Miss Selma had a serious look on her face, and slowly spoke. "Some humans step on us slugs."

"Ouch. I heard about these giants," Lynn spoke in a whisper. "I heard that some humans scoop up slugs and put them in pails a slug can't climb out of."

"Then... they feed... the slugs... to ducks, who eat them up like candy," added Wayne.

Sammy couldn't believe what he heard, and was

afraid to ask more, but he had to know more.... "What's a duck?" Sammy asked.

"It's a kind of bird," said Tina.

Now, Sammy loved birds, but he hadn't thought that he could get eaten by one. This idea made him very uncomfortable, and fearful.

Noticing Sammy's reaction, Tom Tom, piped up, and said, "Some humans if they find us, sprinkle, salt on us."

Sammy was incredulous, and he really didn't want to know anymore, but he had one final question. Fearful of what the answer could be, Sammy bravely asked, "What happens if salt is sprinkled on a slug?"

Everyone fell silent. Miss Selma slowly explained, "It's the worst thing to happen to a slug, and excruciating."

Sammy was too afraid to ask anymore questions.

Tom Tom; anticipating what Sammy's next possible question could be said, "It'll turn a slug into goo!"

"Noooo..." Sammy gasped. He was totally horrified by this news. Sammy couldn't believe all that he had just heard. His mother was always so afraid of humans, and now he knew why.

Tom Tom was about to say something, but Miss Selma stopped him. "Not now Tom Tom. It's time to go over today's lesson."

Miss Selma went over the lesson, and her voice seemed to drone on, and on, to Sammy, as he trembled with fear. Sammy was now totally terrified of humans.

After school finished, Tom Tom slid up to Sammy, and grinned at him. Sammy thought that Tom Tom wanted to play, but instead he asked, "You're afraid of humans, aren't you Sammy?"

Sammy gulped, and was about to say, "No" but

Tom Tom interrupted him.

"You're really yellow," said Tom Tom.

"Of course I'm yellow. I'm a banana, slug," laughed Sammy.

Tom Tom teasingly replied, "No, you're afraid-y-slug, and a show-off."

"No, I'm not," said Sammy, hoping to get Tom Tom off-his-back.

"Prove it!" said Divid.

"What?" said Sammy.

How could Sammy prove that he wasn't afraid? Can you guess?

"Then go under the hedge and eat a cucumber in the human's garden, if you're not afraid," urged Divid.

Tom Tom added, "I dare you to do it, Sammy."

Rosie asked, "What's a cucumber?"

"It looks like a green slug, only rounder," explained Lyn.

"It tastes delicious," Tina said.

Divid continued, "Do it Sammy, and we'll know for sure that you're not afraid of humans."

"I have to go home, now," stammered Sammy. He slid away, as fast as he could go.

"Bye Sammy," said Tina.

To School Or Not To School?

Sammy surprised his mother by coming home early.

"So what did you think of school?" asked his mother. When Sammy didn't answer her, she continued speaking, and didn't notice Sammy's mood. "I was thinking about you all day, wondering if you were having a good day? Did you have fun at school Sammy?"

Sammy realized that his mother loved him very much, because she was thinking about him all day. He couldn't bear to tell her the truth that it was the worst day of his life! So before his mother could ask him anything more, Sammy said, "It was fine, I'm going to The Little Woods."

She called after him, "Don't be late for supper."

Sammy felt bad that he had lied to his mother. He had never lied to her before, but he didn't want to upset her. Sammy was still very upset, and fearful, plus he needed to process what had been said at school. He had wanted to make a new friend there so much; but instead, on the first day he was called bad names.

What could Sammy do about his terrible first day of school? Can you guess?

Sammy decided to ask his mother if he could go to Bird and Mammal School instead of Slug School. He thought that maybe the other animals at Bird and Mammal School would like him, and treat him better. Maybe he could make a new friend there.

Also, Sammy decided that he would not tell his mother the truth. That he couldn't go back to face the other slug students at school, because he had lied about being afraid of humans, and he was too terrified of humans to accept the dare.

Sammy's Parents Confer

It was late at night when Sammy's dad came home.

"Sammy's asleep, so we can talk now," said Vi.

"Talk about what?" replied Sam.

"Sam, your son wants to go to Bird and Mammal School!"

"Well, what happened at Slug School today that put that idea into his head?"

"Sammy said that school was fine."

"Well then it must have been okay. I was hoping he'd stay in school long enough to learn to not eat blackberry prickles, like he tried to before."

Sam and Vi laughed, remembering the incident.

"Personally, I think my son is mighty brave to go to Bird and Mammal School," said Sam.

"But he'll be in school with different forest animals, all bigger than him. You don't see any problem with that?" argued Vi.

"I think Sammy's an adventurer like his old dad. He explored Slug School, and now he wants to explore Bird and Mammal School too."

"So, you're okay with our son going to Bird and Mammal School?"

"Yes, whatever makes Sammy happy."

"Okay, then I'll go see Miss Hoot tomorrow, and ask if our son can attend her school!"

"Sounds good."

Bird & Mammal School

Two days had passed by and it was time for Sammy to attend Bird and Mammal School, in the Tall Tree Forest. It was full of very tall trees, and Oregon Grape plants. When they arrived Miss Hoot was waiting to greet Sammy and his mom.

What kind of animal was Miss Hoot? Can you guess?

Miss Hoot was an owl. When Miss Hoot flew toward Sammy, he was afraid of her, and hid behind his mother. Sammy thought Miss Hoot was a duck, and that she might want to eat him.

His mom said, "It's okay Sammy, this is Miss Hoot, a very wise owl, and she's your new teacher."

"Whew," said a very relieved Sammy. He was so happy that she was an owl, and not a duck.

Sammy came out behind his mother, to take a better look at his new teacher. He could see that she had lovely brown feathers, and huge yellow eyes. Sammy thought she was beautiful.

"Sammy, come say hi to Miss Hoot," said his mom.

"Hi," said a smiling Sammy.

"Nice to meet you Sammy," replied Miss Hoot.

Sammy's mom waved good-bye, and left the school.

Miss Hoot called out, "Students come out here, and meet our new student, Sammy."

Sammy had never been so close to such large animals before. They came out to meet him.

Miss Hoot introduced them one by one: "This is Wilf (fox); Doris (peacock); Pat (badger); Kathe (raccoon); Lois (porcupine); Tammy (quail); Georgey (deer), and lastly, Elaine (bunny)." Elaine looked familiar to Sammy.

What was it about the bunny that was familiar to Sammy? Can you guess?

He wondered if he had met the bunny on The Bunny Trail. He didn't know if it was the same bunny or not.

"Class this is Sammy. Say hello to him," said Miss Hoot.

"Hi," they all said in unison.

"Hi," replied Sammy.

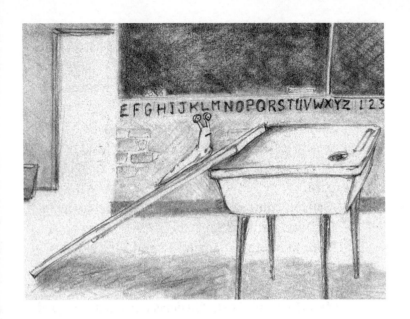

"Sammy, I made a special desk for you. I hope that you like it," explained Miss Hoot.

"Thanks," said Sammy.

What was so special about Sammy's desk? Can you guess?

"Come inside students, it's time for class," called Miss Hoot.

Sammy waited for everyone else to go inside, before entering himself. Once inside, Sammy noticed that every desk was taken; except for one. The desk had a long ramp, leaning against it. Sammy headed towards it, noticing that everyone was watching him, which made him nervous. Miss Hoot saw that Sammy was nervous, so she smiled reassuringly at him. This encouraged Sammy to climb up the ramp. Very slowly he went up, up, up, the ramp, to the top of the desk.

Sammy had an excellent view of the classroom, and was at the same level as everyone else, despite being the smallest student. At last, Sammy felt like an equal to all the other students.

Sammy looked closer at the other students. He thought that Tammy, the quail, had pretty feathers, and he couldn't take his eyes off Doris the peacock. She was the most beautiful bird he had ever seen.

After class Sammy waited for everyone to leave before he descended the ramp.

What do you think happened next? Can you guess?

Miss Hoot went out the back way, leaving Sammy all alone, except for Elaine the bunny, who stood just outside the door.

Sammy tried moving down the ramp but his slime made it very slippery. So slippery that Sammy began to slide downwards, picking up more, and more, speed as he went. Sammy went so fast that he flew off the ramp, and out the doorway, landing on something soft, and fluffy.

What did he land on? Can you guess?

Sammy had landed on top of Elaine, the bunny.

"Ewww... I've been slimed!" Elaine screamed.

"That voice is the same voice I heard on the bunny trail say, 'Ewww...a slug!' Elaine is the same bunny. I knew there was something familiar about her," thought Sammy.

Elaine the bunny, shouted at Sammy, "Get off me, you, yucky, disgusting, pile of goo!"

Sammy was totally mortified by her words, and slid off.

"Ewh, I'm all covered in yucky slime! I wish you'd never come to school today!" screamed Elaine.

Sammy couldn't listen to anymore yelling, and slowly moved away, but was stopped by Doris the peacock.

"Don't let Elaine bother you, she's a real whiner. I think you're brave, coming to a new school today. It wasn't easy," said Doris.

Pat, the badger, spoke up, "Elaine makes it sound like it's the end of the world to get a little bit of your slime on one's self, but it's not. I think it's pretty funny." Pat had laughed hysterically when he saw the sliming occur.

Then Wilf the fox laughed too, and then Tammy the quail; joined by Kathe the raccoon; Lois the porcupine, and Georgey the deer. They all laughed so hard, they fell down on the ground, and began rolling around.

All of the students laughed, except for Elaine, who was fuming mad as she glared at Sammy. Sammy was very hurt by what she yelled at him, and how she called him names.

Sammy felt awful. And though he was very small, he felt even smaller, because of Elaine the bunny's, behavior. While they were rolling on the ground laughing, a humiliated, and hurt, Sammy, slid away, ever so quietly.

Only Elaine the bunny noticed him leave, and shouted after him, "Don't ever come back here - you slime bucket!"

A Friend, At Last

It was getting very windy when Sammy arrived at
The Little Woods. He was so upset that he began talking to
himself, not realizing that he wasn't alone. "I feel so
humiliated... they were all laughing at me... the bunny I
landed on, and slimed, was really soft... but she gave me the
most awful looks, and said the most awful things to me... she
said she wished I'd never gone to Bird and Mammal School
today... I wish I'd never gone to Bird and Mammal School
today, too... and I wish I'd never gone to Slug School either.
Today was the worst day of my life... and I thought Slug
School was bad... they called me names there too... All I
wanted was to make a friend... to play with... Nobody wants
to be my friend...They only want to laugh and call me names

Nobody wants to be my friend."

Just then, Sammy thought he heard a small voice say, "I'll be your friend."

"It must have just been the wind I heard. Nobody wants to be my friend," mumbled Sammy.

But Sammy heard the voice once again say, "I'll be your friend." Followed by a little "Sigh," coming from behind a bush.

"Someone's hiding behind that bush, and they must have been listening to me talking to myself," thought Sammy. *"Could it really be true, could someone behind that bush, really want to be my friend?"*

Who's hiding behind the bush? Can you guess?

Sammy was afraid, but he managed to speak up boldly. "If there's someone behind that bush, come out where I can see you."

The bush began to rustle, and Sammy was even more afraid, but he courageously said, "I know slug karate, you know." Sammy tried to let whoever was behind the voice in the bush, think that he wasn't afraid. Just then, a black and white animal came slowly out from behind the bush.

What kind of animal was it? Can you guess?

"It's a skunk!" said Sammy, loudly.

"I'm a spotted skunk, actually," said the female skunk. She had a sprig of Queen Anne's Lace tucked, behind her ear, and then she remarked "So you know, slug karate, eh?"

"I guess I was a little afraid, when I said that," said

22

Sammy, sheepishly.

"Well, I guess I was a little afraid too, hiding behind that bush," the skunk said.

"But you're a skunk, how could you be afraid of me, a little slug?"

"I've never met a slug before, and you could slime me, like you did the bunny!"

"Oh, so you were listening to everything I said out loud?"

"My name is Sarah-Jane," said the skunk.

"Did you really mean it?" asked Sammy. "Do you really want to be my friend?"

"Yes," replied Sarah-Jane.

Sammy was thrilled.

"What's your name?" asked Sarah-Jane.

"Look, I'll show you," said Sammy, who quickly slid around in circles for a bit, and then stopped to say, "I wrote my initials with my slime trail."

Sarah-Jane came closer to take a better look at Sammy's slimy message. "S.T.S. that's really cool," said Sarah-Jane.

"You, really, think so," replied a beaming Sammy.

"Yes, what does S.T.S. stand for?"

"It's my initials, Sammy The Slug. I leave it behind, wherever I go."

"That's really clever."

"Wow! you're the only one besides me that likes it."

"I like you, Sammy."

"You like me, and you really want to be my friend, even though I'm a slug?"

"Yes," said Sarah-Jane. "Do you like me, and want to be my friend; even though I'm a skunk?"

"Oh, yes," said a beaming Sammy. "I prayed that

God would give me a friend to play with, and now he has."

"Why, I prayed for a friend to play with, too," added Sarah-Jane.

"Thank you God for answering both our prayers."

"What game would you like to play, Sammy?"

Sammy didn't answer Sarah-Jane right away. He noticed the wind growing much stronger. He could see the fir trees blowing wildly, back and forth. Then it happened. Sammy got a big idea, for such a small slug.

What was Sammy's idea? Can you, guess?

With A Little Help From My Friend

"I wonder if you can feel the wind blowing if you climb up on one of those tree branches, and if it would blow you back and forth?" asked Sammy.

"I don't know, have you ever tried it before?" asked Sarah-Jane.

"No, slugs can't climb trees, because we're all slimy, and slippery."

"I can climb trees."

"I didn't know that skunks can climb trees."

"I'm a spotted skunk, and spotted skunks can climb trees."

"That's clever."

Sarah-Jane smiled at Sammy.

"You should climb up into one of those fir trees, onto a branch, and see if you can feel the wind blowing you, Sarah-Jane," said Sammy.

"You should come up into one of the trees with me Sammy, after all it was your idea."

24

"But how?" asked Samy, "I'll slide off."

"You could climb onto my paw, and I'll lift you up onto my back, so that you can slide off. Then after you are safely on my back, you could hold onto my tail, while I climb up the tree."

"Are you serious? You actually want a slimy slug, like me, to ride on your back?"

"Yes."

Sarah-Jane lay down on the ground beside Sammy, and put out her paw. She told Sammy to climb onto her paw, and that she would then lift him up onto her back.

Sammy, obediently, slid onto her extended black paw. Next, Sarah-Jane gently, and carefully, lifted Sammy up, putting her paw down on her back, so Sammy could slide off. Sarah-Jane said to Sammy, "Grab onto my tail."

Sammy leaned back, and grabbed Sarah-Jane's bushy tail with his eyes, because slugs don't have hands to grab with.

"Ok now, hold on tight, as I'm going to climb up a fir tree," warned Sarah-Jane.

Sarah-Jane walked to the fir tree, wildly blowing in the wind.

"This is fun," shouted Sammy.

"I'm glad you're enjoying the ride so far. Let's see if you enjoy the climb up the tree with me. Up, we go," Sarah-Jane, excitedly, called out.

Sammy held on with all the strength of his two eyeballs.

Up, up, up, Sarah-Jane climbed, until she almost reached the top of the tree.

"That's so much fun," said Sammy.

"I'm glad you had fun riding on my back up into the tree. Now I'll lie down on this branch and we'll see if we can feel the wind blow," Sarah-Jane slowly lay down, and before either of them could say anything; the branch they were perched on began to move. The tree swayed, back, and forth.

"Wheeee...," said Sammy.

"Wheeee…," said Sarah-Jane. As the wind gusts blew the two friends wildly about, they held on for dear life.

They were so overflowing with joy that they both began giggling with glee as they rode the wild and windy tree branch together.

Their giggling was carried on the wind, and heard by Sammy's mother. "That sounds to me like my son's giggling, but he's still at school; so it must just be the wind," Vi murmured.

Sammy, and Sarah-Jane, rode the windy branch for a long time, until the wind died down, and they were tired of giggling. Then Sarah-Jane safely, and carefully, climbed down the tree to the ground. Once there, Sarah-Jane lay down, and Sammy let go of her tail, sliding off into the forest underbrush.

Sammy gushed, "That was the most fun I have ever had."

"Me too."

"Best day ever."

"Yes," said Sarah-Jane, "I thought I heard you say earlier, that today was your worst day ever?"

"It was until I met you Sarah-Jane. You're the best friend ever."

Sarah-Jane smiled, and said, "You're my best friend too."

The Two Friends Commiserate

"So will you go back to Bird and Mammal School, tomorrow?" asked Sarah-Jane.

"No, way," said Sammy. "I had bad experiences at both schools that I went to."

Sarah-Jane told Sammy she heard him talking about it when she was hiding in the bush. She heard everything Sammy said.

Sammy felt ashamed, and looked down, not saying anything.

"It's okay Sammy. I understand how difficult it was for you. I had a bad experience at Bird and Mammal School too, and I didn't go back."

What happened to Sarah-Jane? Can you guess?

"Georgey deer wanted to fight Wilf fox; as he is always ready to fight any animal that he comes in contact with. That Georgey, is a real fighter. Anyhow, Wilf fox, was trying to get away from Georgey, who had challenged him to a fight. So, when Wilf was trying to get away from Georgey; he tripped and fell against me; while I had my back turned."

What happened? Can you, guess?

"Skunk's release their scent when they are in danger, and when Georgey fell against me; I released my scent, automatically. Wilf was able to scramble out of the way, but Miss Hoot was standing right behind him, and I accidentally sprayed her."

Sammy laughed outloud when he heard this.

"Then Miss Hoot got really angry with me, as skunk scent smells terrible! So I ran away, afraid that she'd punish me. I heard later that she closed the school for a couple of days, as skunk scent lasts for several days."

"You sprayed the teacher!" exclaimed Sammy.

"Yes, by accident; and after that I was too embarrassed, and afraid, to go back to school," said Sarah-Jane.

"And I thought I had the monopoly on bad school experiences."

"I guess we've both had our share of bad experiences."

"I'm sorry you had such a bad experience at School."

"I'm sorry that you had bad experiences at school, too," said Sarah-Jane. "Are you sure that you're not going back to Slug School, or Bird and Mammal School?"

"Oh, I could never go back to either school, unless," Sammy's voice trailed off.

"Unless what?"

"I have to go home now," said Sammy.

"But you haven't answered my question?"

What did Sammy mean? Can you guess?

Sammy came up with a plan. "Let's meet here, tomorrow morning. I'll tell my mother that I'm going to school, but meet with you instead. I'll answer your question then."

"I'll look forward to seeing you tomorrow," said Sarah-Jane.

"Me too. Bye, Sarah-Jane."

"Bye Sammy."

The Plot Thickens

A smiling Sammy came home triumphantly saying, "I had the best day ever. I made a new friend."

Sammy's mom was thrilled for Sammy, and replied, "I'm very happy to hear that you had a great day, and made a new friend. Your Dad will be very happy to hear that too. I'll tell him when he arrives home tonight. What's your friend's name, Sammy?"

"Sarah-Jane," replied Sammy.

"So, what kind of leaves do you want to eat for supper tonight?" asked his mom.

"Blackberry leaves. I learned how to eat them, and not the prickles, at Slug School."

"Good, your Dad will be pleased."

Best Laid Plans

The next day Sammy waited for Sarah-Jane under the tree that they had climbed. Sammy looked up at the branches, remembering how much fun he had had.

Sarah-Jane rounded the corner noticing Sammy staring up. "It was fun wasn't it, Sammy. You were very brave riding on my back yesterday. Do you want to do it again today?"

"Oh yes," Sammy replied, startled by the sound of Sarah-Jane's voice. "I do want to do it again. But it's not that windy today."

"You never did answer my question yesterday."

"Oh that. Do you really think I was brave yesterday?"

"Yes, Sammy."

"I am brave?"

"Yes," said Sarah-Jane.

"Brave enough to... eat... a cucumber!"

"Do what?" Sarah-Jane was puzzled. "A cucumber?"

"I'll explain it on the way... come with me Sarah-Jane."

"Okay."

"Where are we going?"

Can you guess?

Sammy approached the hedge, leaving his signature behind in his slime. He turned around, and whispered to Sarah-Jane, "We're here."

"Why are you whispering? Where are we?"

"Shhh... I don't want them to hear us."

"Who could hear us?"

"The slug school is just over there, behind that tree."

"Why did you bring me here?" Sarah-Jane asked.

"I'm going to show them all at school, that I'm not afraid of humans."

"By doing what?"

"By eating a cucumber."

"I don't see any cucumbers."

"They're on the other side of the hedge."

"Why would eating a cucumber make you brave?"

"Why? Because the cucumbers are in a human garden!" said Sammy, trembling with fear.

"Humans!" gasped Sarah-Jane.

"You can't be serious about going over there, and you want me to go with you?"

"Nooo... I have to go alone. It's the only way that I can prove to the slugs at school that I'm not afraid of humans."

"Afraid – Sammy it's perfectly normal to be afraid of humans. I'm afraid of humans too."

"Really?".

"I'm sure that the slugs at your school are afraid of human's too, but they won't admit to it."

"You could be right, Sarah-Jane, but I can't show my face at slug school until I eat a cucumber in the human's garden."

"I'm guessing that they dared you to do it, and you're determined to do it alone, eh?"

"Yes," said Sammy.

"So why did you ask me to come with you?"

"Because you're my best friend, whose support I value. I want you to tell the slugs at slug school that I was brave enough to go under the hedge."

"If this is really what you want me to do; then I would be glad to support you this way."

"It is – thank you very much, Sarah-Jane," said Sammy.

"I think you're very, very, brave."

"Thanks Sarah-Jane, Here I go,"   Sammy concluded, and disappeared under the hedge.

Sammy didn't know what to expect on the other side of the hedge. He was relieved not to see any humans. Sammy had his eyes peeled, looking for a cucumber, so that he could taste one, and then get out of there, fast. Sammy spotted rows of green leaves that he had not seen before, and decided to concentrate his search there. He approached a large green object and took a bite out of it. Sammy was surprised that it had red flesh inside, and sticky black seeds. It had a sweet taste, but Sammy didn't care for it.

"Too sweet, and too big, to be a cucumber,"

thought Sammy.

So Sammy decided to taste every round vegetable that he encountered, looking for the one that looked, and tasted, just right. After awhile, Sammy had spit out most of what he had tasted. Finding everything he ate to be: too round, too big, too soft, too hard, or too sweet to be a cucumber. Finally, Sammy came to a round vegetable that fit the description of a cucumber. He approached the vegetable, and found its smell was intoxicating. He took a bite. He had never tasted anything, so good before. *"This must be a cucumber,"* thought Sammy. He enjoyed eating it so much, that he gorged himself on cucumber after cucumber, until he was stuffed and could hardly move.

Suddenly, he felt an odd sensation, and realized that the ground was vibrating. Then he heard a booming voice, say "Ewww…a slug!" Sammy looked in the direction that the voice had come from, and the sight he saw, froze him in place.

"Oh, nooo… a giant… human!" Sammy thought. He was too petrified to move.

What did Sammy do? Can you guess?

Sammy released his only weapon, a foul-tasting slime, to ward off the human. As he waited in terror, he prayed the human would go away. Sammy feared he was going to be eaten, stepped on, or worse, but, suddenly, to Sammy's great relief, the human walked away.

He felt exhilarated, for he had encountered a human, and lived to tell the story. His only weapon, had worked.

"I can't wait to tell the slug's at school, what a brave slug I am. I'm not an afraid-y-slug, I'm brave. Human's, are afraid of me, not me afraid of them. I'm powerful," thought Sammy. For the first time in his life he was all puffed up with selfish pride.

The ground moved beneath him. *"Oh, no,"* thought Sammy *"the human's coming back. My weapon didn't work."* Sammy's bravado was gone.

Wondering what to do next, Sammy heard a booming voice say: "I'm going to put salt on the slug, to see if it really, works."

"Salt – Nooo…" thought terrified Sammy The ground shook stronger, more and more, as the human approached him. "Nooo… stop!" prayed Sammy.

Then it appeared that Sammy's prayer had been answered. The human stopped a short distance away. What looked like snow, fell down from the human's giant hand, onto the ground below. It was too far off for Sammy to see.

The voice said, "Hey, it really works on slugs. But it's really gross though, and what a way to die."

Sammy was relieved it wasn't him the human had salted first; but another slug on the other side of the cucumber patch.

"It could have been me," thought Sammy, shaking with fear. He didn't know what to do next. His slime hadn't worked on the human, and now he was probably the next to face a horrible death. Death by salt would be the most agonizing way for a slug to die.

Sarah-Jane watched the events unfolding. *"Why aren't you moving, Sammy?"* she thought, and yelled, "Sammy, get out of there, now!" loud enough for Sammy to hear, but Sammy still didn't move.

The human moved closer, and closer, to Sammy, but Sammy was frozen with terror.

What happened next? Can you guess?

Sammy prayed, "Oh please drop the salt shaker before you get to me."

Then it appeared that Sammy's prayer was answered, as the human stopped. He felt a whooshing go by him, and a blur of black and white.

He heard the human's booming voice screaming, "Nooo...!!!"

But it was too late. Sammy heard the sound of the salt shaker hitting the ground, and the vibration of the human running away. Sammy wondered, *"What just happened?"*

Can you guess?

The smell of a very pungent odor filled the air, as Sammy heard a familiar voice say, "Let's go, Sammy. That human's going to be busy for a while trying to get rid of the foul-smelling liquid I sprayed on her."

"Thank you for saving my life; you're the best friend ever!" said Sammy.

"You're very welcome Sammy. Did you eat a cucumber?"

"Oh yes, they're delicious, and I ate lots of them."

"That's good Sammy. Now, let's go," said Sarah-Jane.

Sammy left his initials behind him as he crawled under the hedge.

It was pouring rain when Sammy and Sarah-Jane got to the other side of the trail.

"Let's go to the Little Woods Sarah-Jane, if it keeps raining like this we could..." said Sammy, not finishing his sentence.

What could Sammy want to do? Can you guess?

Where's Sammy?

Miss Hoot visited Sammy's mom, to see why her son hadn't shown up for Bird and Mammal School.

"I don't know where Sammy could be, unless he went to Slug School. He said that he had a great day at your school yesterday, and made a new friend named Sarah-Jane."

"What?"

"There was an incident at my school yesterday, that prompted your son to leave school abruptly," explained Miss Hoot.

"Please tell me all about it, while we walk to Slug

School, to see if my son is there?"

Vi and Miss Hoot were joined by Miss Selma, when they arrived at Slug School.

"No, Sammy wasn't at school today?" said Miss Selma.

Just then, Sammy's mother noticed a slug trail leading under a nearby hedge. "Sammy's been here, I recognize his slime signature," exclaimed Vi.

"I don't understand why he didn't come to class," said Miss Selma.

The trio were suddenly interrupted by Tina, the slug, who had overheard their conversation. She told them she thought Sammy went on the other side of the hedge, to eat a cucumber, and that Tom Tom, had dared him to do it.

"Oh no, I told him not to go over there," replied Vi. "I sure hope my Sammy's safe." She moved closer to the hedge, saying, "I'm going over there to see if my Sammy's okay, and if he's still there."

"We'll go with you Vi," exclaimed Miss Selma. With her eye, she pointed at Tina. "You, go home now!"

The trio went under the hedge together. When they arrived on the other side, Miss Selma asked, "What is that terrible smell?"

"There's another animal's footprints here, beside Sammy's slime trail," Vi pointed out. "They double-back under the hedge. I think that Sammy and this other animal are traveling together." Vi paused to glance from side to side. "I wonder if the other set of footprints belong to Sammy's friend Sarah-Jane? Come to think of it, I don't even know what kind of animal Sammy's friend is?"

Miss Hoot turned her head almost fully around, as only an owl is able to, and looked down at Vi. "I'm sure that he's okay, but I'll go with you to make sure."

"Me too," said Miss Selma.

"I wonder what happened to my Sammy while he was over here?" asked Vi.

"I have a theory about it. I'll tell on the way," said Miss Hoot.

Meanwhile, back at the Little Woods, the rain cmae down in a torrential downpour, and formed a waterfall. Sammy led Sarah-Jane to see this spectacular sight.

"I have an idea for a new game to play," said Sammy.

What was Sammy's idea? Can you guess?

"I've always wanted to go under a waterfall and come out the other side, but I can't swim," said Sammy.

"Let's do it together. I can swim, while you ride on my back. The water's not too deep yet, so you should keep pretty-dry,"

"Wow! Sarah-Jane, You can do anything."

"So can you Sammy. All things are possible with God," said Sarah-Jane.

Sarah-Jane lay her paw down so Sammy could slide onto it. And just like the last time she helped him, carefully lifting Sammy up, placing her paw on her back, so that Sammy could slide off.

"Grab hold of my tail and hold on," said Sarah-Jane. And as before, Sammy grabbed a hold of her tail with his eyes. Sarah-Jane climbed carefully down to the edge of the river. The rain changed to a gentle mist. "Hold on tight, I'm going to jump in the river now."

Sammy held on for dear life, as Sarah-Jane splashed

into the river, and swam toward the waterfall. Sammy found swimming with Sarah-Jane a most peaceful experience; one that he didn't want to end. "This is so much fun, Sarah-Jane."

"I'm glad, you are having fun. Now, hold on as we go under the falls."

Sammy and Sarah-Jane disappeared under the falls, and popped out a few seconds later; both, giggling hysterically.

"That was the funnest – ride- ever! And I had nothing to fear," exclaimed Sammy.

"What were you afraid of Sammy?"

"I was afraid of getting washed off your back by the waterfall. But we didn't get wet, because of the cave behind the waterfall."

"But you went anyway, because you are courageous, just like you were when we climbed the tree together, and when you faced the human."

"I trusted you Sarah-Jane, and I'm learning to trust; Creator, God. I bet when those slugs at school find out what I did - facing the human - that they won't call me names anymore."

"You know we left in such a hurry today, I forgot to stop and tell the students at your school how brave you were."

"Can you go and tell them tomorrow? Right now I want to go under the waterfall, again, as it's the most fun ever!" exclaimed Sammy.

So Sammy and Sarah-Jane went under the waterfall, again, and again; giggling with glee every time they came out the other side. Now unbeknownst to Sammy, and Sarah-Jane; their giggling was heard by Vi, Miss Selma, and Miss Hoot; who were not far off. They came to investigate. The trio, were curious about the giggling noises, and were hoping to find Sammy. What they saw stopped them in their tracks.

"It's incredible," said Miss Selma.

"Who'd have thought it possible…?" said Miss Hoot.

"Oh Sammy, you're okay, and I can't believe you're doing what I see you doing," said Vi.

Sammy giggled so much, and was having so much fun, that he didn't even hear the trio's voices, or notice he was being watched.

"He's having so much fun that my Sammy hasn't heard or seen me," said Vi.

"Maybe we should go quietly, so as not to disturb their play," said Miss Hoot.

"That's a good idea. I never thought I'd see the day when I'd see a slug riding on a skunk's back,' said Miss Selma.

"Who'd have thought that my Sammy would. I'm just so glad my son's okay," said Vi.

"I'd say, that he's more than okay," added Miss Selma.

As the trio crept away, Miss Hoot whispered, "I think it's wonderful that Sammy and Sarah-Jane have become such good friends. And what a good friend Sarah-Jane is, to carry Sammy around on her back."

"Who'd have thought that a slug, and skunk, could become friends," said Miss Selma.

"Why ever not?" asked Miss Hoot.

Miss Selma changed the subject. "The other students at my school were picking on Sammy, and I didn't know about it until today."

"I didn't know about it either, and I'm Sammy's mom," said Vi.

"They made fun of Sammy at my school too, and he didn't come back today," said Miss Hoot.

"They were teasing, and making fun of Sammy, at

both schools. I didn't know about any of this. All Sammy told me was that he made a new friend. It must have been awful for my Sammy to be made fun of in two schools," said Vi.

"Sammy does seem to have an extraordinary friendship with Sarah-Jane," said Miss Hoot. "Sarah-Jane used to be one of my students, and I lost my temper during class. And I set a bad example of extolling the virtues: patience, and forgiveness, for my students to follow. I'm so ashamed of my failings as a teacher."

"Don't be too hard on yourself. None of us are perfect. We all make mistakes. I didn't do a very good job teaching my students about kindness, and inclusion," confessed Miss Selma.

"Maybe we could teach a joint class about what, Sammy, and Sarah-Jane, have learned without us teaching them," said Miss Hoot.

What was the lesson that Sammy and Sarah-Jane learned together? Can you guess?

"What lesson are you talking about?" asked Vi.

"Loving one another, despite our differences," replied Miss Hoot.

Miss Selma spoke up. "I think teaching a joint class is a great idea. We never did find out what really happened to Sammy, and Sarah-Jane, on the other side of the hedge?"

Miss Hoot piped up, "Only Sammy and Sarah-Jane know what really happened, and unless they enlighten us about it, we'll never know the truth."

Loyal Friend

The next day before Slug School started Sarah-Jane came up behind the slug students, who were all gathered together talking about Sammy.

"Sammy's not a-fraidy-slug, because he went on the other side of the hedge yesterday, like Tom Tom dared him to!" said Tina.

"How do you know that Sammy went under the hedge?" asked Tom Tom.

"His mom recognized his slime initials leading under the hedge, when she came to find Sammy." said Tina.

"But how do you know that he actually went into the human's garden?" asked a skeptical Tom Tom.

"Well I... don't know for sure," said Tina.

Sarah-Jane who had been listening in on their conversation spoke up: "I know for sure that Sammy went into the humans garden, as I was with him yesterday when he did it."

"What?" said Divid.

"A skunk's talking to us," said a shocked Lady Di-Ann.

"A skunk? Let me, out of here," said Tom Tom.

But before Tom Tom could leave, Sarah-Jane said, "Don't worry, you're safe with me. I'm Sarah-Jane, Sammy's friend."

"Sammy's friend?" asked Lynn.

Lady Di spoke up, saying, "What? Who ever heard of a slug having a friend who's a ... "

"A Skunk," said Sarah-Jane. "Yes, I'm a skunk, alright, and I'm Sammy's friend too. I was with Sammy when he went under the hedge into the human's garden."

"I can't believe it," said Divid.

"I never thought he'd really do it," said Tom Tom.

"Well Sammy did it, and he ate a few cucumbers while he was there," bragged Sarah-Jane. "And he said they were really delicious."

"Wowee! He really did it," said Rosie.

"I told you Tom Tom: that Sammy's no scaredy-slug," said Tina.

"That's right. Sammy's no scaredy-slug, for sure. Actually, he's a very brave, and courageous, slug," said Sarah-Jane.

"Courageous? Brave? Sammy?" asked an incredulous, Tom Tom.

"Yes, he is, and not just because he ate a cucumber in a human's garden, which takes real, guts. But he faced a human, stood his ground, and then slimed the human, chasing her away," said Sarah-Jane, proudly.

"That's unbelievable!" said Rosie.

"Sammy really did all that?" asked Tom Tom.

"Yes, he did," replied Sarah-Jane.

"Sammy really is brave, and courageous," said Lyn.

"Yes, and he risked his life to prove to all of you, that he's not afraid of humans," said Sarah-Jane. "Sammy saw a human, and actually scared it away with his foul tasting slime."

"He did a brave thing," said Lady Di-Ann.

"I wish I could have seen that," said Wayne.

"We were all wrong about Sammy," Lynn added.

"Well, Tom Tom sure was wrong about Sammy," said Tina.

Everyone looked at Tom Tom.

"Alright, alright, I guess I was wrong about Sammy," confessed Tom Tom.

They waited for Tom Tom to continue on and ask for forgiveness. But this was an idea unknown to him.

Meanwhile, Miss Selma, who had been listening in on the conversation, broke the uncomfortable silence by saying, "Time for class. Oh, I see, we have a guest."

Sarah-Jane turned to greet Miss Selma. "Hi, I'm Sarah-Jane, Sammy's friend. Nice to meet you."

As they turned to walk into class, Tina thanked Sarah-Jane for coming to tell them about Sammy's bravery, saying, "I guess we were all too hard on him."

The slug students went back to class. An embarrassed Tom Tom, and a smiling Miss Selma, were the last to enter.

Sammy, and Sarah-Jane, met up again in The Little Woods. Sarah-Jane told Sammy how she told the slug students about his encounter with the humans, and what she left out of the story.

"Why didn't you tell them that you scared the human away by spraying her?"

"Because I think you were very brave to go into the human's garden, and you rode on my back, too. No one needs to know anything other than what I told them. It will be our little secret."

"But... But that makes you a liar, and God says we shouldn't tell lies."

"Even if it's to help someone else?"

"Even then," Sammy slid closer to Sarah-Jane and patted her fur with his eye. "Thank you for being my friend. Part of a good friendship is telling the truth. You've got to tell them what really happened on the other side of the hedge."

"I do?" replied Sarah-Jane talking more to herself than Sammy. "I do," she said, nodding. "You're right, I shouldn't have lied."

Back at the Slug School, the trio met to compare notes.

What do you think they said to each other? Can you guess?

"My Sammy didn't say anything to me about his adventures yesterday," said Vi.

"I'm not surprised. Sarah-Jane came to school this morning and told my students that Sammy scared away the human by releasing a foul tasting liquid," said Miss Selma.

"I didn't know that worked on humans," said Vi.

"What?" said Miss Hoot.

"Slug's secrete a thin layer of bad tasting slime to fend off predators," explained Miss Selma.

"It's our only protection," said Vi. "I can't imagine it scaring off a human."

"Oh," said Miss Hoot.

"I'd say that Sarah-Jane is a fabulous friend."

"I think that the two friends are very fortunate to have found each other, but I believe there's more to this story than what we've been told," said Miss Hoot.

Miss Selma nodded. "The next time I see Sarah-Jane I'll ask her if she had a part to play in scaring off the human. I know how much they fear skunk spray."

"When I told my husband what our Sammy was up to yesterday, he was beaming with pride. We're just happy that Sammy's okay, and that he has an excellent friend in Sarah-Jane," said Vi.

Miss Selma asked Miss Hoot when they would have

the first joint class.

"Tomorrow, I think that your students will be more comfortable at your school," replied Miss Hoot.

"Yes. We can have the class lesson outside under the tree. As there won't be room for your bigger students in my slug sized classroom," suggested Miss Selma.

"Splendid idea," said Miss Hoot.

"What about Sammy, and Sarah-Jane?" asked Vi.

Miss Hoot thought for a moment and then said, "I think that Sammy will come back to Slug School soon enough; now that he's proven to be a courageous slug."

Vi, undeterred said, "And what about Sarah-Jane? Are you going to apologize to her, and ask for her forgiveness for getting so upset when she accidentally sprayed you, Hoot-y dear?"

Miss Hoot appeared all flustered, and she fluffed her feathers. Then she quietly replied, "I'll take care of it, Viola."

Changing the subject, Miss Selma said, smiling, "So, Hooty, we had better have a brainstorm session about our joint lesson. Vi, we'll let you know how it all turns out."

Visitors

The next day Miss Selma told her students that they would be having visitors later in the week. She encouraged them to be respectful of their guests, and not to be afraid of them.

Miss Hoot had a similar discussion with her students, adding that they should be careful to not step on them. Then she also told her students to treat the slug students with respect. Georgey deer, and Elaine bunny, were warned to be on their best behaviour: "No fighting or whining allowed!"

Normally, forest birds and mammals look down on slugs, literally, and figuratively, due to the difference in size. Some birds and mammals can't stand the slime the slugs secrete when they attempt to eat slugs, as part of their normal diet. In such cases, bird or mammal will spit them out. So it's no wonder that slug's are fearful to these other species.

On the arranged day, and at the appointed time, Miss Selma led her students outside of the classroom, and lined them up on the right side of a tree to receive their visitors. They took up their positions just before Miss Hoot, and her students arrived. With them both lined up facing each other Miss Selma directed her students to say hello to Miss Hoot's Students.

The slug students were hesitant at first. This was the first time hey had ever been so close to such large birds and mammals.

Tom Tom remembered that he was told by his teacher, not to be afraid of these animals, but he found it hard not to. It was a challenge for him to even look at them. But he and his fellow students meekly obeyed, saying a weak, "Hello."

Miss Hoot's class replied in unisen, "Hi!"

Miss Selma introduced the lesson saying, "Miss Hoot and I are going to take turns, telling a story passed down from generation to generation through our animal ancestors."

Creator God

Miss Hoot then began "God, our creator, who loves all creatures, saw a long, long, time ago that humans were wicked, and he repented for making them."

"I'm sorry that he made human's too," Tom Tom interrupted, "because they've killed a lot of my relatives by mowing down their homes to make room for their human dwellings."

"Human's have killed a lot of my relatives too, by hunting them with dogs. I hate dogs, and I hate humans." added Wilf the fox.

All the students chimed in together, "Me too!".

Miss Selma scolded them, "Now, students, please, let Miss Hoot continue with her story."

Miss Hoot cleared her throat, and continued, "Because God was so displeased with humans he planned to destroy them... the beasts, every creeping thing and the fowls of the air by a flood...God told a human, Noah, to build an ark... bringing into the ark, two of every kind of creatures...male and female to keep them alive... pairs of all the living creatures entered the ark. It rained 40 days, and 40 nights, and every living creature not inside the ark perished from the face of the earth."

Miss Selma continued the story: "Only Noah, his family and the animals in the ark were saved...after the waters receded... Noah took out every living creature, birds, mammals, reptiles, and insects, to be fruitful and multiply God loved the creatures so much that he saved them by bringing them into the ark... He saved owls, quail, peacocks, foxes, deer, porcupines, raccoons, bunnies, badgers, etc..."

Watching the joint class from a distance, stood Sarah-Jane, with Sammy, riding on her back. Close enough to hear the story, they stayed behind a tree so no one would notice their presense.

"Did he save slugs?" asked Elaine bunny.

"Yes, he saved creatures that move a long the ground, including slugs, even though they are one of the lowliest and humble creatures. God cares even for the slugs and cares for all creatures, equally!"

"Yes!" exclaimed Wayne. "I'm surprised that the creatures would go into the ark with the humans."

"They must have been so afraid!" added Pat, the badger.

Miss Selma continued to tell the reast of the story. "After the creatures came out of the ark God made fear and dread fall on the creatures, and everything that lives, and moves, is food for humans!"

"Oooooo..." the students all gasped, fear striking their very hearts.

"God made us afraid of humans, and it's a natural response for us to feel, whenever we encounter them," said Miss Selma.

"Sammy's not afraid of humans, he scared a human away," said Tina.

"Yes, it's true that Sammy is very courageous," said Miss Selma.

"It's also true that because we're food for humans, it's best to stay completely away from them." Georgey deer muttered.

Tammy quail spoke up for him. "Georgey says that he lives near humans. He also said, that though they carry clubs, he's not too afraid of them. Because their too busy chasing little white balls to notice him much. He also said that humans are the silliest people ever. When they find their ball, they always seem to manage to accidentally loose it again!"

Tammy giggled before she continued. "Georgey also said that humans aren't very smart."

"Why did he say that?" asked Miss Selma.

"Because they can only count to four!" replied Tammy, giggling.

"So, will God send a flood again?" asked Kathe, the raccoon.

"No, God promised that whenever there's a rainbow, that's his promise to all living creatures, that he'll not flood the earth again," said Miss Hoot.

"Whew! What a relief" said Doris peacock.

Miss Hoot concluded the lesson, saying, "You see students, God loves all His creatures very much. So much so, that he saved our ancestors who were on the ark. We're their descendants. Because God loves, and values every creature, so much, we should also love, and value every creature, too. That includes loving, and valuing every bird, every animal, and every slug you encounter. We show we love and value others, by being kind, forgiving, and including them in our activities. This is how we please God, the creator," explained Miss Hoot.

Sarah-Jane stepped out from where she was hiding behind the tree, interrupting Miss Hoot's lesson. Everyone turned to look at Sarah-Jane, and Sammy, who clung to her back.

"Sarah-Jane! I've been meaning to talk to you," Miss Hoot exclaimed.

"What about?" Sarah-Jane asked, stepping closer to the group.

"To ask for your forgiveness. I was angry with you on your first day of school when you accidentally sprayed me. I said mean things, I shouldn't have."

"I forgive you," Sarah-Jane sniffled. "But I have a confession to make too. I lied to you all about how Sammy scared away the human. It was my noxious spray that actually did it."

"It's true!" shouted Sammy. "Sarah-Jane's the real hero. She saved me from getting salted."

Miss Hoot hopped closer to Sarah-Jane. "I forgive you Sarah-Jane. It takes much courage to tell the truth like you just did, especially with such a big crowd of peers around."

"Thanks," Sarah-Jane replied, with her head humbly tilted down.

After a moment of silence, all the creatures shouted, "We forgive you too!"

All the animals crowded around Sarah-Jane and Sammy. Several of them picked Sammy up onto their shoulders, marching him around like a victor. They all cheered, "Sammy! Sammy! Sammy!"

What did Sammy and Sarah-Jane learn from this experience? Can you guess?

Returning Victors

Sammy came back to Slug School the next day, and was treated like a hero by his classmates. They admired his courage, and invited him to join into their games.

Because Miss Hoot had asked for Sarah-Jane's forgiveness, Sarah-Jane returned to Bird and Mammal

School as well, and had a blast making new friends.

Miss Hoot welcomed Sarah-Jane into her class, and told the students there she thought Sarah-Jane was courageous telling the truth the way she did. She said it took more courage to do that than it did to face a human.

Conclusion

By the end of his life-cycle, Sammy saw all the prayers he made as a youth answered. Sarah-Jane remained his best friend, and as long as Sammy lived, the humans never tore down his home, or those of his other friends in the Land of Plenty.